THE FROG PRINCESS

A Tlingit Legend from Alaska

retold by Eric A. Kimmel

illustrated by Rosanne Litzinger

HOLIDAY HOUSE / New York

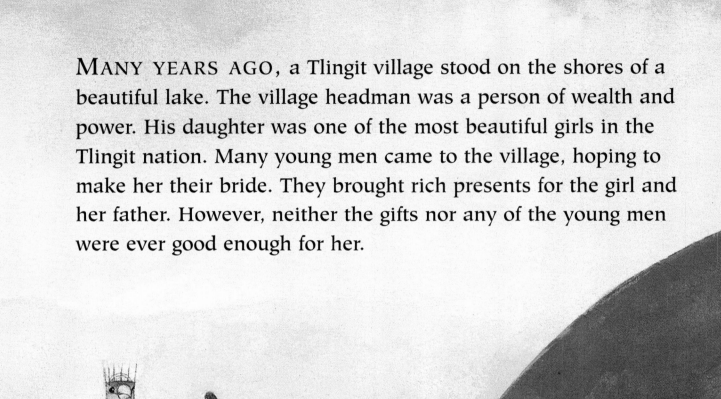

MANY YEARS AGO, a Tlingit village stood on the shores of a beautiful lake. The village headman was a person of wealth and power. His daughter was one of the most beautiful girls in the Tlingit nation. Many young men came to the village, hoping to make her their bride. They brought rich presents for the girl and her father. However, neither the gifts nor any of the young men were ever good enough for her.

"Marry you? Why I would sooner marry a frog from our lake!" she told one suitor whose eyes bulged slightly. Everyone in the village laughed. The poor young man left in disgrace and never returned.

That night the headman's daughter woke from a sound sleep. She heard someone knocking. Dressing quickly, she tiptoed to the door and opened it.

A young man stood on the threshold. A green blanket covered his shoulders. His clothes and fine headdress were also green. The headman's daughter thought he was extremely handsome, though his eyes bulged slightly and his fingers seemed unusually long.

The young man spoke:

"Did you mean what you said this morning, that you would rather marry a frog from the lake than any of the suitors who have come to your village?"

"Yes," the girl replied.

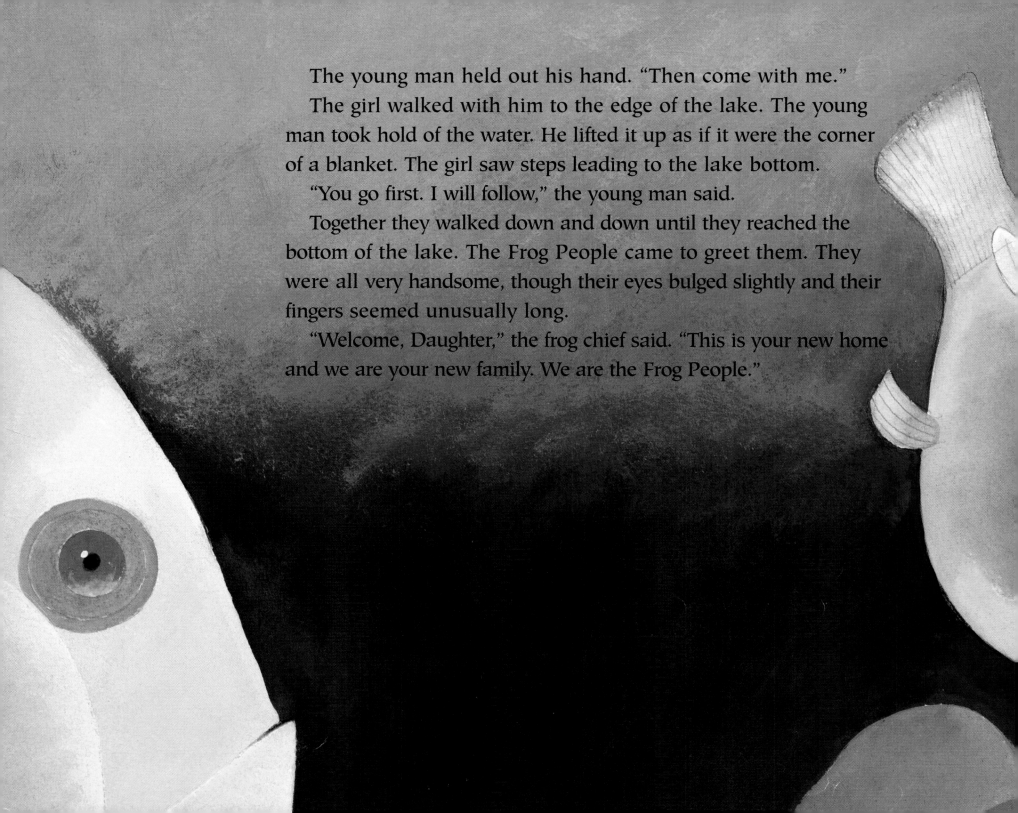

The young man held out his hand. "Then come with me."

The girl walked with him to the edge of the lake. The young man took hold of the water. He lifted it up as if it were the corner of a blanket. The girl saw steps leading to the lake bottom.

"You go first. I will follow," the young man said.

Together they walked down and down until they reached the bottom of the lake. The Frog People came to greet them. They were all very handsome, though their eyes bulged slightly and their fingers seemed unusually long.

"Welcome, Daughter," the frog chief said. "This is your new home and we are your new family. We are the Frog People."

The Frog People led her to a large cedar house. Here they held a wedding feast in her honor. The girl enjoyed the feasting and dancing so much that she forgot about time. Weeks passed. Yet it seemed to the girl that she had been gone only a few hours.

The headman and his wife awoke to find their daughter gone. They searched through the village. They combed the forests and the seashore. They found not a clue. It was as if their daughter had disappeared from the earth. The headman held a funeral feast. The whole village mourned his daughter as if she were dead.

One morning a traveler came to the village. He asked to speak to the headman. He told an unusual story.

"Last night I camped on the far side of the lake. At dusk I heard a young woman's voice singing. I followed the sound. It led me to a marsh. There I saw a beautiful girl sitting on a log, surrounded by frogs. They were all singing and dancing together. This seemed strange to me. Can you explain it?"

The headman asked the traveler to describe the young woman. When he did so, the headman recognized her at once. It was his daughter.

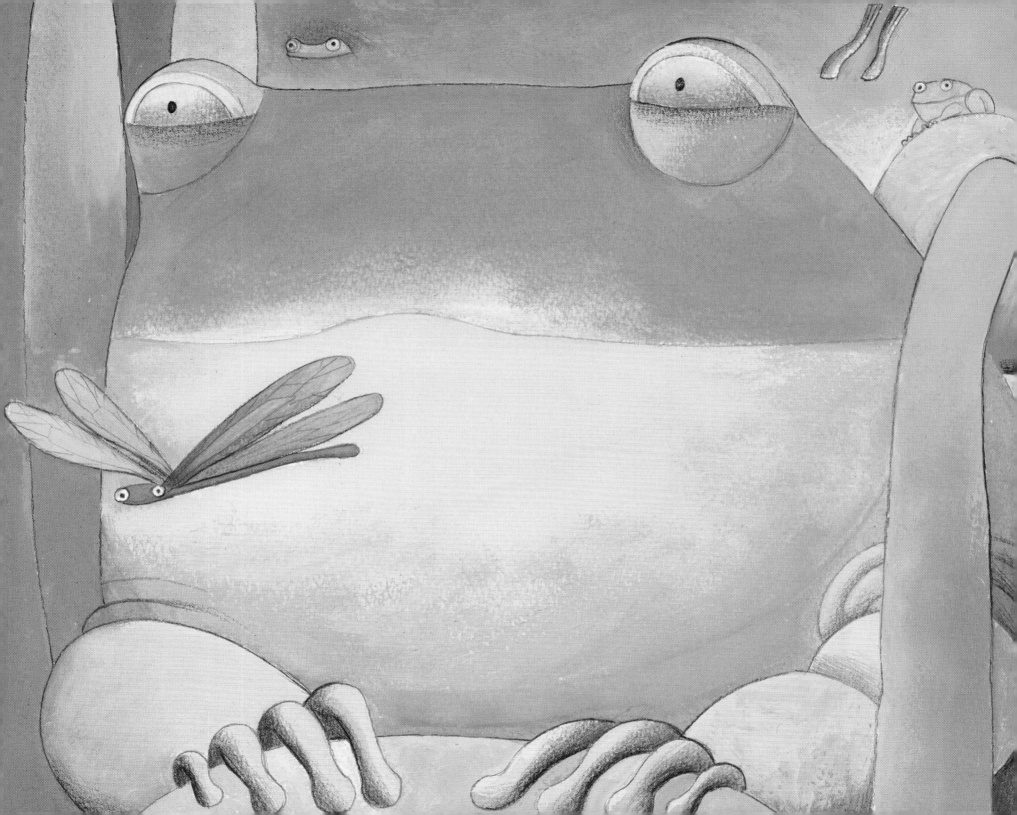

"Take me to the place where you saw these things," he told the traveler. Together they set out for the far side of the lake.

The headman walked along the lake's shore. He stood on the edge of the marsh.

"Chief of the Frog People!" he called out. "Come out of the water. I must speak with you."

The waters of the lake began to stir. A giant frog hopped out onto the beach. "What do you want?" he croaked.

"I want my daughter," the village headman said. "Give her back if she is with you. You have no right to keep her without her parents' consent."

"She is happy with us," the frog chief replied. "She has a husband and many, many children. If you let her stay with us, we will give you great gifts in exchange."

"Keep your gifts. I want my daughter," the headman repeated. "If you do not give her up, there will be war between your people and mine. We will dig ditches to drain this lake. When the water is gone, your people will have to leave. I will find my daughter and take her."

The frog chief blinked his eyes. "The Frog People do not want war. I will bring your daughter back. Return to this spot tomorrow. Your daughter will be here."

The headman went back to the lake the next day. As the frog chief had promised, his daughter stood waiting for him on the beach. She appeared to be in good health, though her eyes bulged slightly and her fingers had grown unusually long. She was dressed in beautiful clothes. A large pile of gifts lay at her feet.

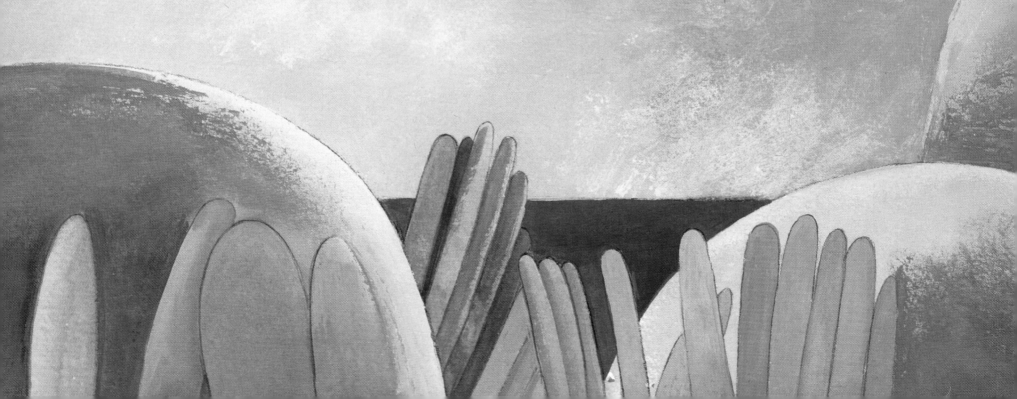

When the headman brought his daughter home, he discovered that she could not speak. The only sounds she made were the croaks of a frog. Her parents prepared a salmon feast in her honor. She did not touch a morsel. She sat with her eyes lowered, looking very sad.

The girl's strange behavior worried her parents. They sent for the shaman. He prepared a healing mixture of roots and herbs to drive out the bad spirits inside her. The girl drank the potion. Suddenly she vomited out a great ball of mud. The shaman broke the ball apart. It was filled with the remains of worms and insects.

"This is the food she ate when she lived with the Frog People," the shaman explained. "Now that she has brought it up, she will be human again."

The shaman's words proved true. The girl looked around, as if she had awakened from a dream. She spoke in human language once more. However, she still seemed sad.

"I was happy at the bottom of the lake," she told her parents. "The Frog People were kind to me. I miss my husband and children. Why did you take me away from them?"

Her parents tried to explain. "We love you too. You are our daughter, and we missed you. It is unnatural for a human girl to live among frogs. They must marry their own kind, and so must you. We will find another husband for you. You will have more children, human children. Forget those frogs. You are back among human beings now, where you belong."

But the girl would not be comforted. Every evening she walked down to the lake. She sat beside its waters, not saying a word.

One day she did not return. The people of her village searched all around the lake. They paddled their canoes back and forth across its waters, but not a trace of her could they find.

The headman went to the lake's shore. Once again he called to the chief of the Frog People. But no one came. The frog chief did not answer his summons. Nor, from that time on, were frogs ever seen in that lake.

But it is also told that once, long after these events, a traveler passing through the mountains camped beside another, hidden lake. That night, as he prepared his dinner, a frog hopped into the light of the campfire. She spoke to him.

"When you come to a certain village, ask to speak to the headman. Tell him that his daughter is well, that she is happy here with her husband and children." Having said these words, the frog jumped back into the water. The traveler saw her no more.

That evening, as the traveler later told the headman, he heard a great number of frogs calling to one another back and forth across the lake. They croaked and peeped, as frogs do. But strange to tell, he added, when he shut his eyes and listened closely, he found he could understand what they were saying. For the frogs were all talking in Tlingit.

AUTHOR'S NOTE

Stories of transformations from human to animal and animal to human can be found all over the world. Readers may wish to compare this story to "The Frog Prince" in *Grimm's Fairy Tales*.

I heard this Tlingit (KLINK-it) story in Sitka, on my first visit to Alaska, in 1995. My version is based on the story "The Girl Who Was Taken by the Frog People" in John E. Smelcer's collection *A Cycle of Myths: Indian Myths from Southeast Alaska* (Anchorage: Salmon Run Press, 1993). Smelcer cites a similar tale collected near Wrangell by John R. Swanton in 1904, appearing in his book *Tlingit Myths and Texts* (Bureau of American Ethnology, 1909).

Other fine books of Tlingit-Haida legends are Mary Beck's two collections: *Shamans and Kushtakas: North Coast Tales of the Supernatural* (Anchorage: Alaska Northwest Books, 1991) and *Heroes and Heroines in Tlingit-Haida Legend* (Anchorage: Alaska Northwest Books, 1989).

To Regina   E. A. K.

For artist Siobhan—with love   R. L.

ARTIST'S NOTE

To the Tlingit and many other indigenous people around the globe, frogs were heralds of abundance and were strongly connected to water and the moon, as well as to emotions. It was believed that frogs could change the weather with the sound of their voices, and their call was known as the "call of the waters." Those listening were stirred and reminded that a change in the climate of their own life was possible too. Able to live on both land and in water, frogs were used as totems for a very powerful process in nature called metamorphosis.

If you are Tlingit, then you are either a Raven or an Eagle, which are the two primary groups in their clan system. I made the Frog Prince a member of the Eagle clan, and as Eagles marry only Ravens and vice versa, I then depicted the Frog Princess and her family as Ravens.

I used red, a color of much significance and importance in Tlingit art, for Frog Princess's father, who is a Raven chief. But I used the sunny and atypical color yellow to distinguish his unusual daughter.

Text copyright © 2006 by Eric A. Kimmel
Illustrations copyright © 2006 by Rosanne Litzinger
All Rights Reserved
Printed in the United States of America
The art for this book was rendered with opaque and transparent watercolors on fine 140-lb. watercolor paper.
The text typeface is Hiroshige.
www.holidayhouse.com
First Edition

1 3 5 7 9 10 8 6 4 2
Library of Congress Cataloging-in-Publication Data
Kimmel, Eric A.
The frog princess : a Tlingit legend from Alaska / retold by Eric A. Kimmel ; illustrated by Rosanne Litzinger.— 1st ed.
p. cm.
Summary: After rejecting all of her human suitors, the beautiful daughter of a Tlingit tribal leader declares
that she would rather marry a frog from the lake.
ISBN 0-8234-1618-6
1. Tlingit Indians—Folklore. 2. Tales—Alaska. [1. Tlingit Indians—Folklore. 2. Frogs—Folklore.
3. Indians of North America—Alaska—Folklore. 4. Folklore—Alaska.] I. Litzinger, Rosanne, ill. II. Title.
E99.T6K56 2006
398.2′089′9727—dc22
2004049347
ISBN-13: 978-0-8234-1618-9
ISBN-10: 0-8234-1618-6